Tales from **EDGEWOOD** The World's Weirdest Town

THE Pawsöns
move in

by Brian & Josie Parker

edited by Sean Fishback

BELIEVE IN WONDER
PUBLISHING

BEAVERTON · OREGON

Welcome to EDGEWOOD.

It is a small, normal looking town at first glance.
However, look a little closer and you'll discover a place
where weird and wonderous things happen everyday.

All rights reserved. Published in the United States by
Believe In Wonder Publishing, Beaverton, OR.

Book designed and illustration by Brian W. Parker, BFA, MA
Edited by Sean Fishback

Inside text set in Life Savers

BIW "reading boy" logo is a trademark of Believe In Wonder Publishing, LLC

Printed in the U.S.A
For bulk orders, event booking, and questions about publishing services,
please email us at believeinwonderpublishing@gmail.com

ISBN-13: 9781726789035

BISAC: Juvenile Fiction > Monsters
Juvenile Fiction > Family > General

First Edition

Summary: The Pawsons, a family of loveable monsters, move into the town
of Edgewood, bringing their own quirky way of being good neighbors.

Believe In Wonder is a family-owned, youth focused publishing company
based in Beaverton, OR. We delight in promoting imagination, inspiration,
and positive thinking in kids and adults alike, and strive to bring diverse char-
acters and new worlds to readers and art lovers everywhere.

Visit us at **believeinwonder.com** for more books, art, and event updates.

For our community

Meet the Pawsons!

They're new in town.
The dad is Barry, and the
mom is Jody, and their sons
are Zip and Maury.

The whole family are very excited to move into their new house in the town of Edgewood.

That night they stayed up talking about all the things they would do their first days in their new place.

NOT JUST TREATS, ZIP. WE NEED TO GET FOOD.

They made their first trip to the store. The Pawsons made sure to get everything they needed...

BUT I WANT FRUIT SNACKS!

...and they got a **LOT** of groceries.

They took their dog Ruff
for a walk around the
neighborhood...

...and had some interesting interactions with their new neighbors.

They went to the park to have some fun...

....and it may have gotten a little bit out of hand.

The Pawsons loved to go out for breakfast, so they had to find a new place to get pancakes...

As usual, it didn't go as well as expected.

By the end of their first
week, something was
bothering Zip.

So Barry and Jody sat down
with their boys.

IT'S OK IF WE
DON'T QUITE FIT IN.
WE'RE DIFFERENT –
AND DIFFERENT CAN
BE VERY SPECIAL.

Just then, the Pawsons got some unexpected visitors.

They welcomed the Pawsons to the neighborhood and brought them a special treat.

After such a nice visit, the Pawsons' spirits were lifted, and they decided to invite over all of their neighbors.

IT'S SOMETHING SPECIAL WE CAN SHARE WITH OUR NEW FRIENDS!

Barry even brought out the
family grill.

People came from all around, following the smell of hamburgers and the sound of laughter. Everyone had a great time.

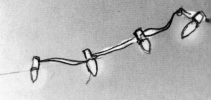

That night the Pawsons cuddled up, full and happy to be in their new home.

It was different, but different can be very special.

The Parkers live in Beaverton, Oregon, and are the owners of Believe In Wonder Publishing.
Their lives and their work are devoted to sharing imagination and creativity with young minds,
and inspiring a new generation of dreamers.

Follow us on Facebook @ www.facebook.com/BelieveInWonder/

PICK UP THESE BOOKS

from BELIEVE IN WONDER PUBLISHING

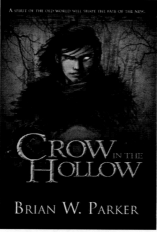

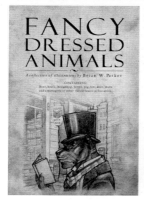

now available on AMAZON.COM

visit WWW.BELIEVEINWONDER.COM

As a special treat...
please enjoy these exclusive coloring pages!

Feel free to copy or scan them, or just color them in the book.

Barry

THE
Pawsöns
move in
© Believe In Wonder Publishing • Beaverton, OR

Jody

Zip and Maury

Made in the USA
Middletown, DE
14 October 2023